The TIDELINGS of DRAS SAYVE

A Prequel Novelette

C B Lansdell

Contents

Armoured Drassyr

Knyadrea: A tidally-locked habitable moon and the setting of this story.

The Dras Channel: Three clans on the far side of Knyadrea, in the northern hemisphere. Dras Rindar is on an island to the south of the channel, while Sayve lies to the north. Dras Nauka is spread over an archipelago between the other two clans. The channel is named after the armoured drassyr, a marine creature.

UNITS OF TIME:

Segment: A period of 24 hours. Informal: *seg*.

Phase: 6 segments.

Revolution: 5 phases and the completion of one day and night cycle.

Year: 14 revolutions.

Segere: The first 9 hours of a segment.

Median: The middle 6 hours of a segment.

Segeind: The last 9 hours of a segment.

UNITS OF MEASUREMENT:

Deget: A small unit of length based on the average knyad's distal phalanx.

Alkar: The length of the average knyad's forearm.

<u>LIFE PHASES:</u>

Polyp: 0–3 revolutions.

Tideling: 3 revolutions–5 years old.

Juvenile: 5–25 years old, after which they are considered adults. Informal: *juve*.

<u>OTHER:</u>

Ae, aer, aerself: Standard pronouns that apply to all knyads.

Andrid: Denotes someone who identifies as male and uses the pronouns he/him.

Gynid: Denotes someone who identifies as female and uses the pronouns she/her.

Kyr: A respectful way of addressing another knyad without using aer name.

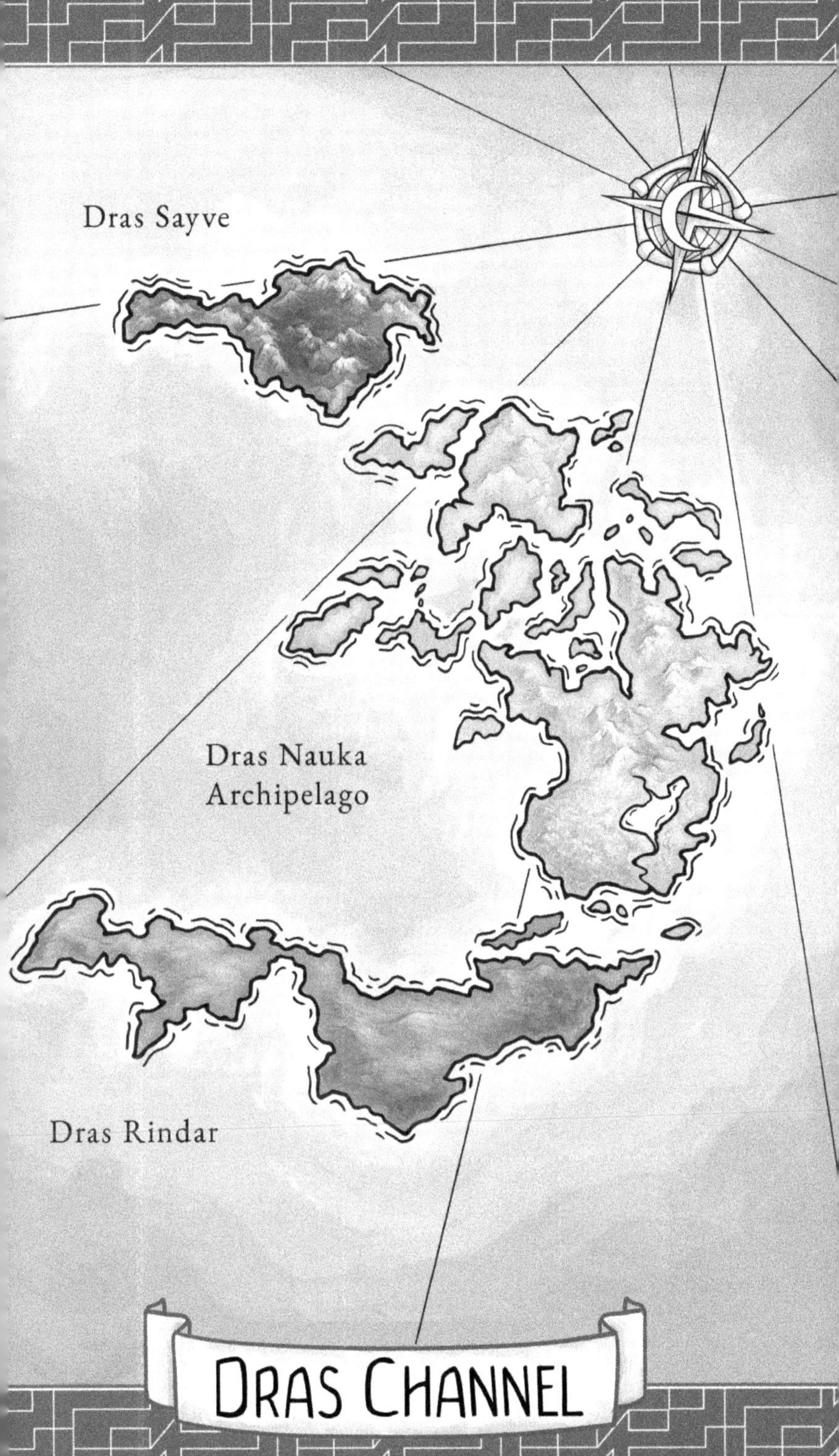

Dras Sayve
Dras Nauka
Archipelago
Dras Rindar
DRAS CHANNEL

To the parents and mentors who try different keys until they unlock stores of potential in the young.

CHAPTER 1

The Elder's Favour

FRIGID, DARK WATERS, MURKY with nutrients, lapped at the hull of the Rindarian Cabin Cruiser. These were the marine conditions Emis had come for. Beyond the wharf, tall, pitted conifers stretched leagues in all directions ...

He had arrived.

Dras Sayve's mountainous landscape formed the coroneted head of the armoured drassyr, the serpentine fish the Channel Clans collectively resembled. Emis had just come from Dras Nauka, the curving, plated body; before that, he had stopped at his home clan, Dras Rindar, the prehensile tail. Neither had much to offer him this time. Though Emis had good relations with clans around the moon, he hoped to avoid extending his search beyond the Dras Channel. A sense of kinship and shared cultural values bound the Drassians. Over the years, Emis had tutored students from all three clans, and they had all gone on to succeed in their chosen careers. But none of them struck him as the person he was waiting for. It would be different this time, in Dras Sayve. His breakthroughs happened here.

The sun remained fixed above the horizon, tinting the white landscape with a warm glow. Here, at the northernmost part of the Channel, the air was especially bracing. Emis had docked his cabin cruiser alongside other recreational watercraft on the forested side of the island, some distance away from the cove that served as the clan's nursery. At the base of the gangway stood a figure dressed in a blue and white padded coat. Emis grinned down at her, and she folded her arms.

Stasia had come into her own as an elder of Dras Sayve. The rippled oval buckle of the cinch belt around her waist signalled her expertise in the field of education. Emis supposed he had also come some way since their time together at the Drassian Academy. Within moments of their first meeting, each had marked the other as a rival. Over time, abrasiveness gave way to mutual respect and admiration. Though Emis was also a teacher of sorts, he had no idea how Stasia managed entire dormitories of rowdy tidelings. Their paths had long since diverged, but neither had quite managed to forget the other. Somehow, she always made time to collect him between mentoring young teachers and advising the peer and governors.

The gangway creaked as he reached the bottom and strolled to Stasia, arms behind his back. She tilted her head back, dark eyes sparking as they met his. Shorter than him by a half-alkar, she was as lithe as he was barrel-chested. Her feathered tendrils were styled in a weightless cut that showed off her delicate chin and nacre-coated earrings. Sayvians placed little value on time-consuming tendril extensions. Even Emis's tendrils, which he fastened with a clip at the back of his head, were longer than hers. Stasia placed her hand over his forearm in greeting, her skin cloudy blue against the vibrant russet of his.

Emis cocked a half smile. 'The welcome party gets smaller each time I come here. Am I to take this as a hint that I should stay away longer?'

She released his arm. 'I almost didn't come to collect you. You arrived a whole segment early.'

'There was nothing left for me to do around Dras Nauka and sailing conditions here were fair.'

She gave a disapproving huff. Raising the hand on which she wore her mitter, she called her assistant to bring a turbine sleigh around before returning to Emis. 'Everyone is a little preoccupied. We have a harvesting cere-mony later this median. You'll just have to join in with the preparations.'

'Another?' He laughed. 'Peers and moons, tidelings are being brought ashore every time I come here. What are you putting in the sea?'

'I'd think you would be pleased about our healthy population, given your reason for coming here.'

They left the icy wharf, their boots meeting softer layers of snow. 'The last protégé I took from Dras Sayve was a juvenile of around eleven,' said Emis. 'I'm considering someone younger this time, a five or six-year-old.'

Stasia curled a finger on her chin. 'Hm, that is young. I will have to speak with the governors about it. They may allow you to take someone who has finished aer foundational education. I'll have Pawel, the Form 5 resident advisor, come to you tomorrow. He knows that age group best.'

The pair reached a clearing at the edge of the forest, where the wharf connected to the mainland, and waited for their transport. Emis sent her a sly smile.

'What?' she asked.

'Remember when we were at the academy, you said you wouldn't trust me to keep algae in a tank alive? Now you're about to send me someone who has barely left tidlinghood. Could it be I have proven myself to you?'

'I wouldn't trust you with the tidelings in the nurs-ery,' she said, raising her eyebrows. 'But juveniles can see to their own needs. They must start thinking of their futures.'

'No one better to prepare them for it than me. As you know, I am all for discipline: early segeinds, exercise, study routines, the lot.'

'It takes leaving their home clans for some to appreciate those lessons.' Stasia wrinkled her sharp nose. 'Much like a Rindarian student I once knew.'

'Maybe my protégé, finding ae has a taste for adventure, won't return home.'

'Then I trust you will groom aer into a respectable representative abroad. Our clan has bright juveniles to spare. If you are offering to accommodate one for us, I won't object.'

Emis shook his head, grinning. 'Oh, you're ruthless, Stasia, luring me here under the pretence of doing me a favour. This arrangement suits you too, doesn't it?'

'I haven't the time to indulge you if there's no benefit for me.' She spoke curtly, but her brown eyes twinkled and she was barely hiding a smile.

'That's fair,' Emis said with a shrug. 'Will there be an opportunity to meet them today – the juveniles?'

'Perhaps. You will stay for the tidelings' dinner this segeind, won't you?'

'A dinner, you say?' He patted his stomach, which didn't quite protrude from his coat. 'It seems I timed my arrival well after all.'

'Some of the younger juveniles will be there,' continued Stasia, 'hopefully on their best behaviour. Tradition requires them to help with the preparations and welcome their new harvestmates.'

A low hum and a pale flurry between the trees heralded the arrival of their turbine sleigh. Emis offered Stasia his hand as she stepped aboard the vehicle. For a moment, he wondered what his life would be like had he laid anchor where she was. Of course, they had always wanted very different things. She'd have found his questionable business decisions and wayward associates trying. No ... his long absences were better for their relationship. Behind him, the turbines whirred to life, interrupting his musings as he settled into his seat. The sleigh glided in a circle, its nose pointed in the direction of the seaside buildings.

CHAPTER 2

The Harvesting Ceremony

A TIDELING WEARING ONLY an aquaskin grabbed the handrail at the water's edge while a carer supported aer free arm as ae emerged from the sea on wobbly legs. With surprising fluency, ae thanked the carer in the land-based language, Collective. So young, and already the tidelings' aptitudes were apparent; some took to walking with ease while others learned to speak sooner.

Emis stood with the elders of Dras Sayve, watching the proceedings from a shaded pavilion overlooking the series of tidal pools that made up the nursery on the eastern side of the cove. Dark clouds gathered over the snow-capped mountains behind them, but the buildings at the coast were washed in gentle, yellow sunshine. Hanging from poles were the blue flags Stasia had him hoist upon his arrival. Emblazoned with intersecting triangles of pale green and silver, they billowed proudly in the chilly breeze.

There were no signs of industry on this side of the island. The harbour lay to the west, far from areas where tidelings were found. Stasia, a few teachers, and the Form 1 dormitory advisor were dressed in elegant tunics of blue and silver over white pants; the nursery staff and other elders wore similarly cool colours. Emis hadn't changed out of his beige coat, but he blended in with the group. He could be more distracting on another occasion; this was the tidelings' segment.

Despite having witnessed many harvesting ceremonies since his own some fifty years ago, the awe never left Emis. Each new knyad was a miracle, a gift from the sea, bursting with potential. Only a year ago, the currents had carried these very tidelings here as spongy, curled polyps, no bigger than Emis's fist. Now, many of them stood at the shoulder height of their adult carers.

He turned to Stasia and asked, 'Were all the tidelings found in this cove or are some from your neighbours?'

'We haven't raised Nauka's tidelings in years,' she replied. 'Not since they opened additional nurseries.'

Dras Nauka, the most populous clan in the channel, was fractured, spreading over several islands. A local carer had once told Emis they had to check even rocky islets for signs of polyps.

Emis gave an impressed huff. 'A robust-looking group, aren't they? You have excellent carers.'

The Sayvians were fortunate to have so many developing polyps washing into their catchment areas when most clans' populations had dwindled. The cold currents feeding Dras Sayve's coastline likely contributed to their healthy numbers. Today, the clan welcomed seven tidelings into Form 1.

Carers bundled the tidelings in layers of blankets. Though the seawater's chill had not yet left their blood, they wrapped their rangy limbs over their chests, warding off the biting air. Gradually, their round cheeks flushed with colour. It was difficult to tell them apart; their stubbly tendrils would only start growing after they left the water. The tidelings' skins rippled, mimicking the ribbed texture of the towels around their shoulders before smoothing out. Underwater, camouflage was a necessary adaptation for such vulnerable creatures. It would be another three years before their appearances completely stabilised.

Clouds of air puffed from their mouths and noses. With their lungs fully developed, the gills in their necks were starting to shrivel closed. Some of the tidelings may have been ready to leave for phases already. Dras Sayve usually held their harvesting ceremonies every three revolutions, during a high tide, so there were enough tidelings to justify the effort.

Heads and webbed hands bobbed above the waves as other tidelings, who were not yet old enough to leave the water, watched their friends graduate to Form 1. Some of the newly harvested looked bewildered, others excited. One of the swaddled tidelings looked at the sea with a contemplative expression. Though they would remain adept swimmers throughout their lives, they would never again live underwater.

As the last tideling left the water, Emis turned his attention to the uniformed young knyads welcoming their new harvest mates. The fifth-formers, now virtually the same height as the adults, were considered juveniles rather than tidelings. Though still fresh-faced, their features and colouring had settled, and some bore defined markings.

A white and grey fifth-former with a brusque manner directed the newcomers to the changing rooms. Another yawned and leaned against a flagpole while his neighbours talked among themselves, oblivious to their new harvest-mates.

But something intriguing was happening at the back of the line. Like short-finned yunulae seeking the slipstream of a watercraft, a few tidelings trailed a slender juvenile. Seemingly untethered from the ground, ae was tugged this way and that by the activity around aer. Though aer skin was not vividly coloured – somewhere between grey and blue – aer face appeared bright. Ae wore aer mussed tendrils in an overgrown version of the standard Sayvian cuts. Rather than ordering the tidelings about, ae inclined aer head to listen to them before responding animatedly.

Stasia caught Emis's eye.

'Who is that juvenile?' he asked, tipping his head towards the scene below.

'The one directing the tidelings is Edurne. She's firmer with them than some of the dormitory staff.'

'No, I meant the fleet-footed one at the back.'

'Oh?' Stasia craned her neck to look and, upon noticing the friendly youth, gave a sighing laugh. 'That's Oklas. Popular with the young ones, isn't he?'

'You can see why. Watch how he adjusts to each of them.'

She nodded. 'You'll have the chance to speak with him tomorrow, along with the other fifth-formers.'

The last of the tidelings, followed by the juveniles, disappeared into the changing rooms. Soon after, one of the younger teachers cornered Emis, barraging him with questions about his travels, while the elders whisked Stasia away for a meeting. Every knyad here seemed intent on preventing them from having a moment alone together before the dinner.

A Seat at the Table

F LAVOURFUL STEAM FROM THE kitchens greeted Emis as he entered the darkened foyer, leaving behind a crisp, bright segeind. The scent goaded a growl from his stomach. After raising all those flags and banners, he had worked up an appetite. The Old Town Hall, with its burnished glow and folk art carvings, seemed out of place amid the sleek, colourless buildings surrounding it. The handsome bowed shape of the hall's interior reminded Emis of the hull of a giant wooden vessel. Paper decorations in the colours of the flags at the cove covered the timber walls and tables.

A juvenile ushered him past a group of teachers and elders to the far end of the hall, showing him to a long table where Stasia sat, chatting with a colleague. Further along the table sat the wide-eyed tidelings, dried and clothed in Form 1 uniforms. Emis could have sworn three had left the water with pale thread-like patterns on their skins, but now it seemed only one tideling bore noticeable markings. They must have changed since then. In no time, they would be mimicking each other's features to trick their dormitory monitors.

They were a lively group, with many bouncing in place, unable to contain their excitement at the sights, smells, and textures of the world above the waves. Although one had fixed aer hands firmly over aer ears to shut it all out.

As everyone began to take their places, something about those seated near Emis struck him as unusual.

'Stas,' he said quietly, leaning over to her ear. 'Is it customary for the nobility to attend every welcome dinner?'

Stasia smiled. 'No, we don't usually have this many. They're here to meet the newest heir presumptive. One of the tidelings harvested today was discovered during a meteor shower.'

According to Sayvian tradition, the unusual celestial occurrence would mark this tideling as the eleventh member of Dras Sayve's nobility. Most praemor clans devised similarly random criteria to identify heir presumptives. On Dras Rindar, they were the tidelings who, as polyps, had washed in with severe storms. Some Praemor raised their nobility to lead, but the Dras Channel clans elected their governors on merit, grooming their presumptives instead to become custodians of culture. While senior presumptives inherited estates and performed ceremonial duties, their young counterparts studied and worked like everyone else.

Positioned near the peer's table, it appeared Emis was considered an esteemed guest. Or perhaps Stasia had altered the arrangement so she could have the pleasure of his company for the segeind. To Emis's left sat a foam-grey knyad, Valenska, one of the senior presumptives. Dressed in an elegant off-white suit, Valenska didn't wear any further ornamentation to display his seniority, as was fashionable among nobles further south. He was a little older than Emis but rumours suggested he kept to the Dras Channel, having travelled abroad only once in all his years.

Peer Olensia Sayve stood on the other side of the hall, wearing an expression of polite interest as she met with the new tidclings. A dark-skinned, elderly knyad, her posture was still upright as a striaspruce sapling. However, Emis had heard she was preparing the senior presumptives to take her place in the next few years. The governors would ultimately decide which of them would succeed her as Clan Peer.

Aside from their initial greetings, Valenska said little to Emis until after both had finished their glazed seafrond starters. 'So, Emis, is business still taking you south of the Channel?' he asked.

'Oh, it takes me everywhere,' he replied. 'I was sailing planet-side only two revolutions ago.'

'Our new ambassador, Osura, tells me you recently declined an offer to serve as a minister in the General Assembly.'

'I was tempted, but the timing wasn't right. I'm not ready to settle in one place for that long.'

Frowning, Valenska nodded. 'Apidecca is becoming too overcrowded. Best we leave the Erudean Pentarchy to manage their ancient stronghold.'

'Should the opportunity come up again, I may take it,' said Emis, offering his and Valenska's plates to a juvenile collecting crockery. 'There's no better vantage point for keeping a sharp eye on the Eruds.'

Valenska dismissed the notion with a wave. 'They won't pass any laws to disadvantage us – they need the support of the Praemor if they hope to control the hoards. I hear the Assembly is struggling to find uses for all the Orta arriving in the city.'

Emis stroked the barbs around his chin. 'They'd be arriving here in the Channel if we weren't so far from the Nebbian and Litusian continents. They may yet decide we're worth the journey.'

'How reassuring, then, that we have our Rindarian watchers safeguarding us at the bottom of the Channel,' said Valenska, filling Emis's goblet with a splash of Mindalill wine.

'It wouldn't do for us to chase away our trading partners,' cautioned Emis with a laugh. 'Some of the Orta have become successful enough that they are now considered equal to the Praemor.'

'Good. They are developing as they should. Perhaps they can supply us with more raw materials?'

There was a great deal of interest in the few quality inventions Dras Sayve released to market. More often than not, they outsourced production to Dras Rindar. As a young knyad, Emis had made his fortune brokering trade deals on Sayve's behalf. But the Sayvians held back a great deal, even from their neighbours.

Emis gave a genial huff and told Valenska, 'If the other clans knew what you are capable of, they'd be clambering to invest here. It isn't easy advertising the works of such a secretive people.'

'There's no need for us to become too friendly with our trading partners. Praemor clans who lose their way soon find their cities overrun with immigrants.'

'Lose their way?' repeated Emis, bemused.

'They become greedy, compromising their integrity so they can extend their reach,' said Valenska, tapping the table for emphasis.

Emis looked into the clear green-tinged depths of his wine glass. He couldn't help himself. Some views begged to be gently challenged. 'Desperation more than greed drove them. Some of those older clans were on the decline until Orta immigrants revived them.'

Straightening in his seat, Valenska continued, 'Even so, they will come to regret accepting such assistance. The knyads who arrive in these cosmopolitan cities bring with them a host of different ideas and values. It invites chaos.'

He swiftly drained his wine glass. 'If we in the Channel were to open our borders, we'd have more to lose than to gain. The time of expansion is over. No one is investing in Orta dependencies anymore. Then there are those new clans, the ones that haven't even been assigned a stratum.'

'The unclassified?'

'Is that what they're calling them?' said Valenska dryly. 'The Assembly ought to simply classify them as Orta, and give them some pride in themselves. Otherwise, those knyads will never believe they have something to contribute.'

'Is it any wonder, then, that they want to leave for more prosperous lands?' prompted Emis.

'They must learn to invest in their own clans. We in the Channel had no option but to become self-sufficient, being so far from everyone else. We left our dependencies with more than we had when our clans emerged.' He glanced at the head of the table, where Peer Olesia Sayve sat, then back to Emis. 'The governors and I have told Peer Sayve that she needn't donate so many resources overseas when they would be better spent on needy islands off Dras Nauka.'

Emis could point out that no technologically advanced civilisations had been there to exploit the Channel clans at a vulnerable stage in their development. That even the least of Nauka's islands enjoyed a decent standard of living. Instead, he took a sip of his wine and said, 'The Naukans deserve our support, of course.'

Just then, juveniles flocked into the hall again, this time bearing trays of broth, the first of a few courses.

Emis and Stasia exchanged smiles, his strained and hers apologetic. He felt better knowing he had her sympathy at being placed next to the dour Valenska. He looked up in time to see the friendly juvenile from the harvesting ceremony – Oklas – grinning at them from the other side of the hall.

Emis turned to Valenska. 'It's good to see your juveniles involved in so many Sayvian harvesting traditions.'

'Indeed,' said Valenska, nodding. 'Before they graduate from the dormitories, they must set an example of service and dignity to the new tidelings.'

Still looking at Emis, Oklas leaned past Valenska to serve him his meal. Misjudging the height of the table, he dropped the bowl before the senior presumptive with an unceremonious *plop*. It narrowly avoided tipping over, and steaming oily broth spilt onto Valenska's arm. Attention snapping back to the table, Oklas quickly dabbed at the mess with a cloth, only spreading the stain on Valenska's sleeve further. Blurting an apology, he gave a jerky bow and scurried back towards the kitchens.

It all happened too quickly for Valenska to respond. His jaw dropped, lengthening his already pinched face. Avoiding Emis's eyes, he said gruffly, 'Of course, some require further refining.'

'There's plenty of time for that.' Emis glanced towards Stasia, who was twirling noodles into her spoon, then back to Valenska. 'Your teachers have provided them with a solid foundation.'

'It's best to immerse impressionable tidelings in the culture of their clan, minimising outside influences,' said Valenska, pressing a serviette against his wrist and plucking a stray noodle from his cuff. 'Though I endorse healthy cooperation with one's neighbours, of course.'

He raised his bowl to Emis and, smiling, Emis mirrored the gesture.

The broth was followed with a variety of delectable meats and vegetables, all exquisitely presented. Every now and then, Emis chuckled at the tidelings who found the most creative ways of eating ... with or without the utensils laid out for them. Soon, the tired young knyads were led away to the dormitories. The adults also left the tables, mingling or sitting on the benches lining the sides of the hall, their conversations lasting late into the segeind.

Taking Chances

Footfalls and excited chatter emanated from the Form 5 dormitory stairway and Emis turned around. A young dormitory monitor in a plain blue uniform tried valiantly to keep ahead of the juveniles pouring down the stairs into the common room. It was the median after the harvesting. While the juveniles were in class, Emis had used the segere to prepare the space for them. The fireplace was lit and a few tables had been filled with snacks and drinks – a modest spread compared with last segeind's fare.

'Nasek, don't touch the food just yet,' called the harassed monitor. 'Can I have everyone's attention? Master Emis Rindar, andrid, is visiting us from our neighbouring clan. You don't want to give him the wrong impression of Sayvian juveniles.'

'They can't be much worse than Rindarian juveniles,' said Emis, walking up to the dormitory monitor. He placed a hand on aer shoulder. 'Why don't you take your leave, kyr? I can manage from here.'

The dormitory monitor shot him a grateful look. A juvenile aerself, ae could've hardly been much older than those in aer care. Drawing closer to Emis, ae quietly asked, 'Are you sure you wouldn't like me to stay and introduce you to them one at a time? There's been a lot of excitement recently and they're a bit unruly.'

'Don't trouble yourself. You may watch them from a safe distance – at the refreshments table, perhaps? Find something to eat before they descend on it.'

He returned to the juveniles and they stared at him. If the dormitory monitor hadn't already introduced him, Emis's clothes, stature, and warm complexion would have made it obvious that he wasn't a local. Yesterday, he had blended in with Sayvian neutrals, but today he wore a showy red coat that was more distinctly Rindarian.

'I'm not here to give a lecture; you aren't tidelings any-more. No, I want to thank you. After your efforts at the harvesting ceremony yesterday, I thought you'd earned the median off. I enjoyed your hospitality, and now I can share some Rindarian delicacies with you in turn. I only ask that you stay until I've had a chance to speak with each of you. I have worked in education for a long time and Elder Stasia has kindly allowed me to come here and learn a bit about those of you who are completing your foundationals.' He spread his arms, gesturing towards the table. 'So please, relax. I'll catch up with you later.'

At first, the juveniles remained in place, nervous perhaps that any sudden movements would draw Emis's attention. He left them, joining the dormitory monitor in the corner. Sensing he wasn't about to pull any of them aside, the juveniles started helping themselves to the food and soon seemed to forget he was there. Emis looked among the young faces, but there was no sign of the person he was most eager to meet. No matter. It was too early for him to lock on to a favourite, and he had to take a chance on those here.

Intrigued whispers reached him as he passed groups around the room:

'He is an ambassador from Apidecca.'

'No, he's not. He's a merchant.'

'I heard he owns a whole island near the equator.'

An attractive juvenile with webbed patterns stretching over aer ice-blue skin crossed aer arms, frowning at aer stockier harvestmate, who protested, 'They're real, Bystry. I'm going to show him.'

'That capture is clearly a manipulation,' Bystry replied flatly. 'You want him to think we all believe in conspiracies and imaginary creatures?'

The other juvenile sped through the capture library projected above aer mitter, a metal bracer on aer wrist. 'The source is reliable; it was transmitted from a Pentarchic clan.'

'I do enjoy a good mystery,' said Emis, stepping between them.

The juvenile with the holographic capture turned to Emis. 'You're well travelled, kyr. Have you ever seen a cyclops?'

'A one-eyed knyad?' He skewed his mouth, exaggerating a frown. 'I know someone who lost an eye ... interesting story.'

The juvenile's shoulders fell.

'Unless you're talking about creatures of legend?' prompted Emis in a hushed tone.

'Legend? No.' The juvenile pulled a face. 'But maybe genetic experimentation? It must have gone wrong because this thing is uglier than the underside of a barnacle.' Ae angled aer mitter so Emis could see the projected image. At first, Emis could make out only an inkblot in the murky capture. Then, a most unnatural face came into view.

He took the juvenile's wrist and lowered the display. 'Now, telling a young Sayvian not to pry is the surest way to inflame aer curiosity. Here in the Dras Channel, we favour the sciences over mysticism. Easier to regulate, I suppose. But there are a few who can tap into the supernatural and make distortions of ordinary things. Best we keep our speculations quiet. The Pentarchy don't take kindly to people poring over their secrets.' He gave a knowing smile. It would take someone craftier than a juvenile to investigate the sovereign council. Even Emis had to admit there was still much he didn't know about their grim practices.

His insights had won him the juveniles' regard. The pair introduced themselves to him. The andrid conspiracy theorist was named Jedrik. His gynid harvestmate, Bystry, took it upon herself to share the names of nearby juveniles with a commentary on their areas of aptitude. But she was most interested in the one person in the room she didn't know. 'I saw you sitting near the peer's table last segeind,' she said, tilting her head at Emis. 'Are you a Rindarian heir presumptive?'

He chortled. 'Oh Eruds, no.'

'But you are someone important or you wouldn't have been seated next to Master Valenska.'

'There are other important roles you can assume outside of the peerage.'

'I'm counting on it,' she said with a slight smirk.

'You seem to know all your harvestmates well. Tell me, how many are in Form 5? I'm sure there were more of you at the dinner?'

'Thirty-seven were harvested in our year. We're missing Oklas and Ranek today.'

Another juvenile, Arvid, snorted. 'They had to stay after class to clean up the lab.'

'Master Mirona should have known better than to put those two together on a project,' said Bystry haughtily. 'They get into enough trouble separately.' She leaned closer to Emis, eyes wide, and explained, 'We were studying bioluminescent algae from the panel lamps. Oklas and

Ranek did something to the water – by this segere, all the walls and floors were caked in purple powder.'

'The panels exploded,' said Arvid, shaking his head and grinning.

Emis decided he would check if the missing pair were still at the laboratory when this was over. At the front of the hall, the Form 5 advisor, Pawel, called the dormitory monitor away, leaving Emis alone with the juveniles. They were warming to him, growing louder as they jostled for his notice.

'Ease up, all of you,' he instructed, voice raised. 'One question at a time.'

In the absence of their supervisors, the juveniles were surprisingly capable of organising themselves. They formed a circle around Emis, awaiting their turns to ask their questions:

'How do we know there is no life on Planet Axis?'

'Why are some knyads orange when everything under-water is blue or green?'

'Do Orta knyads speak Collective?'

And so they continued.

A group of quieter juveniles lingered at the edges of the room. For a moment, Emis thought he saw a shock of pale blue tendrils among them. Before he could glance that way again, Edurne, the brusque juvenile from the cove, was in front of him, asking how deep the sea was on Knyadrea's planet side.

After a time, those who did not wish to speak with Emis snuck out, mixing with the juveniles he had already seen. He was starting to appreciate the work it took to keep track of so many. When the last of them left, Emis returned to the monitors' lounge and found himself alone there. The room looked out onto a copse of snow-covered spriastruce trees. From the tall bay windows, dense branches cast long shadows on the hardwood floor.

Funny. One of the shadows looked almost like a knyad in shape.

A lower window pane shot up, and Emis gaped as a lean juvenile sprung into the room. There was no balcony outside; he had to have swung in from a tree or the windowsill.

Emis exhaled hard, his heartbeat slowing. 'That's quite an entrance, juve.'

'I was looking forward to meeting you, kyr. I hope it's not too late for us to talk?' The juvenile held out his arm. 'I'm Oklas, andrid.'

Emis gripped the underside of Oklas's forearm, stating his name and gender identifier in turn. 'So you're the fifth-former with the exploding algae. Care to divulge your methods?'

'They didn't explode so much as burgeon,' said Oklas, scratching the back of his head. 'Ranek wanted to change the chemical composition of the water. She thought it might alter the brightness and colour of the algae. They're mixotrophs, so I suggested feeding them different microorganisms. We introduced a cultured solution to the tanks and, well ... they may have found it a bit too agreeable.' He looked down at his purple-stained fingernails and, grimacing, quietly added, 'Those tiles won't be grey again anytime soon.'

'Scrubbing your classroom clean is a fair trade-off for an entertaining story,' said Emis. 'Though if you're smart about it, you can make some terrific stories without getting caught.' He poked his head through the window and noticed a thick branch curved from the nearest tree against the side of the building. Emis would have easily been able to climb it when he was Oklas's age – assuming the branch could bear his weight. Even then, he had been bulkier than the Sayvian youth. 'So, how long were you waiting outside this window?'

'Since the dormitory advisor left. I couldn't let him see me because' – Oklas looked over his shoulder and back to Emis – 'because I'm not supposed to be back here yet. Ranek and I rushed the cleanup, and the lab still smelled of rotting clams when we left.'

'Hoping to overhear some of your harvestmates' questions, were you?'

Oklas gave a derisive laugh. 'Most of them tend to ask things they could look up on their mitters.'

'And you think you can come up with better than that?' asked Emis, raising his eyebrows.

Pacing the room, Oklas pressed his fingers to his cheek. 'We don't often get visitors who've travelled as extensively as you, so I'd be interested to learn about the things you've seen. Or I might ask what brings you back to the same clans year after year. Clans like Dras Sayve.' He gave a sly smile. 'Maybe it's not something but some*one* you come for?'

Emis feigned a look of mild curiosity. 'Oh? Who might that be?'

'Elder Stasia,' answered Oklas coyly. 'She doesn't stop what she's doing to fetch just anyone from the harbour. Then there were those looks you exchanged at the dinner ...'

'You're good,' conceded Emis. 'Yes, Stas and I go far back. We met when I came here as a juvenile to study at the Drassian Academy. I must admit, it's refreshing to talk to a Sayvian so invested in his elder's social life.' He tilted his head at Oklas, who looked at the sunlit floor.

'My teachers usually call it gossip.'

'You say that like it's something to be ashamed of. Why, gossip is the mortar binding societies,' said Emis, stroking the barbs that covered his chin. 'I'm sure I saw you hovering behind the retiring juveniles at the back of the hall. You aren't shy, are you?'

'Me, shy?' Oklas laughed, flipping his tendrils from his eyes. 'No. I snuck in to ask them if the dormitory monitors were still around. My quieter harvestmates actually have a lot to say; they just don't want to try shouting above Arvid or Bystry. And really, can you blame them?' He pulled a page covered in dense writing from his pocket. 'A few asked me to pass their questions on to you.'

'Go on.'

'Casimir wrote them down – he has the neatest handwriting.'

Emis took the paper from Oklas. 'When I return to my cabin, I will record the answers and send them to you in the segere. However, your friends skipped their chance to speak with me, and you're here now. Why not tell me a bit about yourself, Oklas?'

For once, the juvenile couldn't quickly summon an answer. He took a step back, then flashed a smile. 'There's not much to tell. My harvestmates are probably the ones to ask.'

'You're a fifth-former; it won't be long until you leave the dormitories. Is there a field of study here on Dras Sayve you'd like to enter?'

'Our teachers would have us all working in laboratories. I do enjoy the sciences. It's just ... it's always so quiet in a lab. You spend a long time working in one place.' A cloud fell over him. 'Still, there are emerging technologies that involve more fieldwork. I could become an inventor and start a business. I hear resyn engineering can take you all over the world.'

'You know,' said Emis, ' I started out as a trader before I went into teaching. Both paths prepared me for what I'm doing now.'

'And what is that?'

'Freelancing as a diplomat.' Emis chuckled at Oklas's reaction. 'Don't turn your nose up at it. I know what people say about politicians, but few other careers will afford you encounters with as many different people.'

Oklas gave a subdued smile. 'I guess it's no different from teaching. You're just placating adults instead of tidelings.'

Emis threw his head back and roared with laughter. 'Adults are often easier to trick. Though I don't know that I'd call my preferred tactics "placating".' He winked at Oklas. 'What I enjoy the most is teaching people about my clan and learning about theirs. You also make friends. Friends that can help you in other ventures.'

Stepping back, Emis gave the juvenile an appraising look. 'Tell you what, if you want, why don't you spend the segment with me tomorrow? There's no one better to ask about the newest developments in a town than a young person. I'll have your teachers excuse you.'

Oklas grinned. 'Really?'

'Yes, but I expect to be taken on a guided tour so you'll have to plan our itinerary. Do you think you can do that?'

'Of course.'

'Right, then. I will go and speak with your Advisor Pawel.' He opened the door a crack and checked the landing. 'All clear. Best you go and join the other fifth-formers before anyone spots you in here.'

'Thank you – oh, and kyr?' said Oklas, stopping as Emis held the door open for him. 'I enjoyed our talk.'

'May it be the first of many,' said Emis, patting him on the back and closing the door behind them.

CHAPTER 5

About Town

CRANING HIS NECK, EMIS watched his young companion hanging from the railing at the back of the tram carriage. Oklas was beaming, his tendrils whipping about his face. Dras Sayve's transport network was one of the best in Knyadrea. Their trams were quiet, streamlined, and surprisingly swift for energy-efficient vehicles.

'If you're going to stay outside, you should at least close that door behind you,' called someone plaintively. Emis turned to see another passenger some seats behind him turn aer collar up at aer neck, shooting Oklas an injured look.

'So sorry. It is a bit chilly, isn't it?' said Oklas, running a hand through his tendrils as he reentered the carriage and shut out the draft.

He dropped into the seat next to Emis. Pursing his lips to suppress a naughty smile, his blue eyes flicked to the disgruntled passenger as if to say, *Can you believe how petty they are here?*

Emis wagged a finger at him and put on a comically reproving expression.

Framed by the curved windows of the carriage were scenes of rushing government buildings, research facilities, and shops. Occasionally, a spire punctured the procession of sinuous white lines and arcs. Lining the street were several two-wheeled scramblers and convertible sleighs, some of which had already swapped out their runners for tyres. Most were powered by fulmenum cells, but for the sake of tradition, some were pulled by qintralope: the nimble, hoofed creatures found in this part of the Channel. It was not in the culture of Sayvians to rush anywhere.

'Oh, this is our stop,' said Oklas, already standing with one hand on the seat in front of them. He swayed forwards as the tram braked smoothly.

Emis followed him outside, his boots crunching in the snow. 'Care to share the itinerary yet?' he asked.

'Not all of it at once. I don't want to spoil the surprises.' Oklas looked at a towering white building that resembled a series of layered sails. 'Over there. We're starting with the library.'

The interior of the Sayvian library was more impressive than some of those found in even the Pentarchic clans. Books lined walls four storeys high, reaching the vaulted ceilings. Oklas seemed familiar with every corner of the place, leading Emis under archways to casting laboratories or sliding back shelves concealing holographic presentation rooms – things Emis didn't even know could be found in libraries. Though Emis was a teacher, he had always gained more from lived experiences than trawling through information in places like this. Sayvians were always precious about their books, and Oklas was no exception. The juvenile had a hungry mind, and the places he chose for their tour reflected this.

Next, they walked past a series of research centres some blocks from the library. Emis suspected that Oklas hadn't a firm idea of where they were headed and was merely stringing together a series of unplanned outings as he went along. He would have done the same at that age.

If Dras Rindar was the commercial centre of the Channel, Dras Sayve was its source of scientific innovation. The laboratories they passed pursued a range of goals, from synthesising organic matter to developing cybernetics.

Oklas stopped outside an elegant clinic with a window display of tanks containing corals in varying shades of blue and silver. It was a cloning centre: an insurance policy, should tideling populations in the Channel drop unexpectedly.

'I remember visiting this facility some years ago,' said Emis. 'Back then, they were attempting to grow tideling polyps in a controlled environment. Do you know what became of that generation?'

'They were returned to the nursery at the cove after they showed signs of deterioration,' replied Oklas. 'They needed to be in the sea.'

Emis's expression must have betrayed some concern because Oklas raised his hands reassuringly. 'They're fine now. I'm friends with a couple of them.' The juvenile shifted from one foot to the other, hands in his pockets, and elaborated, 'The clinic mostly takes biopsies from polyps these segs. They hope to grow new tidelings from the samples, but it hasn't yielded results. The corals you see here are all that develop from them.'

'Something must be missing,' said Emis. 'The spark that sets off complex life.'

'Or maybe we should consider the corals knyads?' proposed Oklas. 'We haven't yet devised any tests for sapience in them.'

Emis chuckled. 'They could be listening in on our conversation now.'

Oklas smiled vaguely and stared through the tanks with unfocused eyes.

'You must be proud of your clan's accomplishments,' said Emis. 'Even if they don't find success in this area of research, Dras Sayve is still a leader in cybernetic augmentation.'

'I am proud to be a Sayvian,' replied Oklas, his narrow shoulders hunched as he watched the scientists in sterile suits and breathing masks meticulously going about their work. 'I'm just not sure this is what I want for myself.'

Emis nodded and resisted the urge to pat the juvenile on the shoulder. Oklas looked cold, diminished at the prospect of a future lived on his people's terms. It made Emis all the more sure that he had to be the one to change that.

Emis had assumed Oklas's favourite venue was the library until they reached the planetarium. Here, they lingered the longest.

They stood beside a colourful holographic model depicting the orbital resonance relationship between Knyadrea and Dryadeen. The planet, Axis, appeared as a static ball, while the moons of Knyadrea and, on the periphery, Dryadeen, revolved around it in a hypnotic dance.

'Notice how Knyadrea is tilted at an angle?' said Emis, gesturing to the orb. 'It's slight – barcly felt in most clans around the moon – but enough that we experience some seasonal shifts here.' He pointed to the Dras Channel region in the northern hemisphere. 'When I studied at the academy, I couldn't believe Dras Sayve could be so lush and green in the warmest revolutions.'

'Most Sayvians can't wait for that time of year,' said Ok-las. 'The lunar nights feel more like extended sunsets, and the lake water doesn't ice over. I suppose it is my favourite season too. But there's one thing I like about the cold revolutions.' He looked up at a constellation of sparkling tiles set in the dark ceiling, his eyes full of longing. 'When we're fully turned from the sun, I can see even the stars between stars.'

Emis led Oklas to the planetarium exit, stopping at the cafeteria to fill his flask with kahv. He bought Oklas a stew-stuffed flatbread and one of the sweet hot drinks Sta-sia liked.

When Oklas had finished eating, Emis got up from the table and said, 'Now that you've had your fill, let's do something more active. Tell me, juve, are there any sports you enjoy?'

'I try to make all our skiddering matches to cheer on the juvenile teams,' he replied. 'Not that they need it. They beat Dras Nauka's Northern side constantly. Nasek and Bystry score the most goals, and Kosta is the best trapper – he's also fun to celebrate with afterwards.'

'What about you? Are you on the team?'

Oklas laughed. 'No, I'm more of a recreational player. The others sometimes ask me to join the odd game of kreulleston as a sweeper. I'm not bad at it; the stone usually slides down my paths.'

'Very good, though I don't suppose that's an activity that can be done in pairs?' asked Emis, folding his arms.

Oklas frowned thoughtfully. 'Do you skate, kyr?'

The lake next to the gymnasium would remain frozen solid for some segments, though Emis doubted anyone would be skating across it next phase. All around him and Oklas were coniferous trees and glassy towers – and a few other skaters, mostly older juveniles who had finished their studies for the segment.

Emis's considerable height and broad frame challenged his balance. He took to the ice slowly and centred himself. There it was. Even after some years away, he hadn't forgotten how to negotiate this slippery environment.

Oklas circled him, smirking. 'You're a fair skater for someone from the south of the Channel.'

'I did live here for four years,' Emis reminded the juvenile. 'I used to spend more time here than studying. I couldn't let Stasia better me on the rink now, could I?'

Oklas furrowed his eyebrows, puzzled. 'I can't picture Elder Stasia being that competitive.'

'She is,' said Emis emphatically. 'Fiercely so. She just hides it very well.'

Four juveniles waved to Oklas from the other side of the lake. They were dressed in coats of different styles and colours rather than the blue uniforms worn by those still in the dormitories. Oklas excused himself to join them. For a while, they skated and talked. Then Oklas broke away from the group. Emis watched him zip around the lake, the blades of his skates tracking glistening threads in the ice. The juvenile rose from the mist hovering over the lake, a spirit of air and frost. He wasn't the fastest or most forceful skater, and he often seemed unaware of his surroundings, darting and skidding to avoid collisions, but even these jarring movements he executed with a casual flair. The wind whipped about him, catching his lithe limbs as it did flurries of snow.

Oklas returned to Emis, exhaling clouds of vapour, his cheeks aglow. Together they skated to the lake's edge and sat on a bench under an arch of goldbristle vines. Oklas explained that the juveniles he had spoken with were only a little older than him. Having graduated from Form 5 a year earlier, they now stayed in the town centre.

Clenching his jaw, the juve tried to keep himself from shivering. He was wearing only a light jacket over his dormitory-issued casual clothes.

'See the part of the gymnasium roof overhanging the lake?' he said, pointing to the section of the building hiding behind the curtain of coarse vine leaves. 'Last year, Ranek, Casimir, and I climbed onto it from the tower above. We laid down a fluted shaft and piped water from the tower to make a slide.'

'With that incline, you must have shot down there at speed,' remarked Emis, impressed.

'We spent a whole segere sliding into the lake before anyone noticed. The Form 4 advisor wouldn't let us leave the dormitory courtyard for the rest of that light phase.' Oklas chuckled, then coughed. 'Foznits,' he said shakily, wrapping his arms around himself.

'Not so warm when you stop moving, is it? Here.' Emis took off his coat and raised it above Oklas's shoulders.

'Oh, I couldn't—'

'I've plenty of padding, and the kahv has warmed me enough.'

'Thank you,' said Oklas, slipping his arms into the oversized sleeves. The wine-coloured cuffs almost covered the length of his hands. 'When you're gliding over the ice, do you ever feel like you may just leave the ground? Fly into Axis on the other side of those mountains?'

'Now that'd be an adventure.' Emis sat back and sipped from his steaming flask. 'Do you often think of travel?'

'All the time. I'm not going to work here my whole life.'

'Nah,' agreed Emis, 'When I saw you, I thought to myself, "This one has the look of someone who wants to touch the horizon".'

'That I can do from anywhere,' said Oklas, extending his fingers so they covered the line where the sky met the land. He tilted his head all the way back. 'But I want to come up higher.'

'I can't promise you the stars,' said Emis, 'but perhaps I can help you find your own way to them?'

Oklas's lips twitched, and he asked, 'What do you mean?'

'There's a city just south of the equator – sail that coastline in the middle of a dark phase, and all you see above and below, reflected in the water, are constellations. Even the light of Axis doesn't reach that far.'

'Is that Knyadrea's capital?'

'Apidecca, yes. Of course, you won't see much of the sky once you're in the city. Most of it is either underground or in the shadow of the gorge. If you haven't anything planned after your foundational education, I might invite you along on one of my trips there.'

'Really?' Oklas's eyes widened.

Emis shrugged. 'I can always do with a spry juvenile onboard to help carry my luggage. Think you can handle that?'

When he was sure Emis wasn't joking, Oklas extended his hand, and Emis gripped the underside of his forearm. 'It's a deal, then.'

They parted there, at the edge of the lake. Oklas didn't have far to travel – the tideling dormitories were close by – and as luck would have it, Emis didn't have far to go either.

CHAPTER 6

The Governors' Conditions

Having CHOSEN HIS CANDIDATE, all that remained was for Emis to meet with a governor
about it. It was a formality; if experience was anything to
go by, the discussion would be brief. Even Stasia was coming to advocate for him, which was a kind gesture. The
board of governors had never objected to Emis's requests
before, and with his record, he gave them no reason to.

He walked past the dormitories, through the courtyard
to a multi-storey building that stretched behind the other
blocks. The staff room was empty for the segeind, though,
adrift in boxy furniture on the porcelain-tiled floor, was
a small gathering. Emis slowed as he approached the dim
corner of the room where not one but three governors
waited for him. Stasia was there too – she looked tired.

Emis recognised Governor Inger, a pleasant knyad who
usually waived procedures for him. But who were the
other two in stiff formalwear? The young governor with
deep-set eyes Emis had seen after the dinner, speaking
with Valenska. Ae was the only one standing. The third
governor was a squat older knyad with a downturned
mouth.

'What's this?' asked Emis, offering a smile that none of
the others returned.

'Master Rindar, please take a seat,' said the severe young
governor, gesturing to the modular sofa where Stasia sat
opposite the others. Ambient light from outside cloaked
the room in grey; the algae panels in the walls behind
the governors glowed blue and yellow, casting spotlights
on canvases depicting textured, geometric shapes. Emis
sat in the middle of the sofa, close to Stasia. He felt like
a tideling appearing before his dormitory advisor after
causing trouble.

'I am Governor Ustal, andrid,' said the serious knyad, taking the seat between his contemporaries. 'This is Governor Inger and Governor Burza, both gynid.' He gestured to the knyads at his left and right, respectively. 'Elder Stasia relayed to us your request to mentor one of our juveniles.'

'Apparently, you have already taken three from Dras Sayve,' said Burza, narrowing her eyes at Emis. 'Do your own people not meet your stringent requirements?'

Emis shook his head. 'I have mentored students from every island in the Channel. I used to teach a few each year, but this time I am offering a position for only one, and ae will have my full attention.'

'It will set a dangerous precedent if we allow you to take a fourth,' said Ustal, pacing slowly, his hands behind his back. 'Our clan seeks to limit the number of juveniles that can be educated outside of Dras Sayve by a particular group or individual.'

'Now, be reasonable,' said Emis, barely tempering the harshness in his voice. 'Governor Inger can attest that I have a long-standing history with Sayvian educators. And any of my previous students will tell you I am a responsible guardian.' *At least*, he thought, *they like me enough to leave out anything too fun for the governors.*

Ustal frowned. 'Stasia tells us your next protégé will be away for over a year. This is longer than we can allow.'

'What? Why?' Emis turned to Stasia, who was looking at her hands folded in her lap.

'Simply put,' said Burza, 'we don't want to begin a trend that will see our young emigrating from Dras Sayve. Already one of your former students, Agota, lives abroad.'

'In a Pentarchic clan. They sought her out for her skills as a surgeon – who would turn down such an offer?' Emis didn't much care for the Pentarchy, but no one could deny it was an honour to earn their praise. 'The other two are still here. Lato returned with knowledge of construction techniques he couldn't have gained here.'

Burza bristled in her seat. 'How could he learn anything from knyads who know nothing about Sayvian architecture? No doubt he imports materials of inferior quality from overseas.'

'Lato is among those protecting our heritage,' said Stasia firmly. 'He is an esteemed restoration architect.'

'Even so, Elder, I am sure you can appreciate that there are many ways in which outside influences can dilute our culture,' said Governor Ustal.

They sound like Valenska. Emis wondered whether the senior presumptive had put the governors up to this. Were they all of the same mind?

He spoke up. 'The Channel clans enjoy Praemor status and an allocation of funds from the Erudean Pentarchy. You want to hold the attention of our world leaders; Dras Sayve needs representatives beyond an ambassador in Apidecca. Isn't it worth preparing a few interested juveniles for intermediary roles?'

'What is your agenda, Emis?' asked Governor Burza sternly. 'Poaching our juveniles, slowly blurring the borders between the Channel clans? Rindarians have always sought to ingratiate themselves with the rest of the world. Maybe you seek favour with the Eruds so all the Channel clans might be unified under Dras Rindar?'

'I've never heard such utter spume,' bellowed Emis, getting to his feet. He might have irreparably impacted diplomatic relations with the Sayvians had Stasia not come between him and the governors.

'That's enough,' she said in a commanding tone that would give even the unruliest tidelings pause. Emis and Burza returned to their seats and, more calmly, Stasia continued, 'The Channel clans are our neighbours, kin. We will not make baseless accusations. Emis respects our ways. I know of a few tidelings that would benefit from his brand of mentorship.'

Governor Ustal, who had paled, cleared his throat and gave Governor Burza a sideways glance. 'We apologise for misjudging you, Emis. Though, it is still for us to approve your choice of candidate. We can't send away our most promising juveniles when many have prospects awaiting them here. Do you have someone in mind?'

'Yes. Oklas,' replied Emis.

Stasia's mouth opened, then closed. The governors frowned at each other uncomprehendingly. Then, Inger addressed Stasia. 'Do you have any impressions of Oklas, Elder? What are aer records like?'

'Oklas performs well across a range of subjects, though he is not among our highest achievers. He would thrive in a less structured environment.'

'So he hasn't yet left the dormitories?' interjected Burza.

'He's a fifth-former, but he will graduate by next revolution,' replied Stasia evenly.

Burza tutted. 'Little more than a tideling. Emis will have to take someone older.'

'No. I will take no one else.'

Ustal gave a weary sigh and clasped his hands. 'Master Rindar, you are fortunate we are allowing you to take anyone at all.'

'Perhaps,' said Inger, 'we could allow Oklas to leave after a waiting period. Ensure the juvenile is exposed to life here before he leaves?'

After a pause of consideration, Governor Ustal said, 'To offset the resources our community has put into raising him, the juvenile owes us at least two years of service.'

'Two years?' repeated Emis incredulously.

'Yes,' said Governor Burza. 'Over that period, he won't be allowed to enrol in another program. It'll only take more of our funds, and there's no guarantee he'll spend his working life here.'

Emis dug his fingers into the edge of the sofa. 'What will he do in that time, languish?'

Burza shrugged. 'There are plenty of menial jobs. He can supervise automated processes as a technician.'

'And we could always use more dormitory monitors,' added Inger helpfully.

'But—'

Stasia gave Emis a silencing stare. 'Thank you, governors. I think that is a fair arrangement.'

It didn't matter what else was said as they ended the meeting. Emis remained quiet – if he said anything more, his temper would get the better of him. He left the room in haste, chest tight and temples throbbing. Stasia followed behind at a more dignified pace until they reached the corridor.

She sprinted to catch up to him. 'Don't do anything rash, Emis. We're not done negotiating.'

'When did your leaders start nosing into people's comings and goings? You'd think I'd been caught smuggling polyps from the cove.' His voice came out gruff, but Emis took care to avert his gaze from Stasia. He'd never take out his frustrations on her. 'And it's ludicrous that a juvenile should owe his clan anything for raising him. I'd be doing them a favour, educating Oklas,' he continued, jabbing at his chest. 'I don't even want his allowance. At this point, I'd bribe them to release him into my care.'

'Keep your voice down,' hissed Stasia. 'If they over-hear us, it won't help matters. We'll talk more when we're home.'

Home. That is what her apartment was to Emis whenev-er he came here. It calmed him, knowing that's where they were headed. 'Thank you for being there, Stas.'

She inclined her head and continued in a low voice. 'It's not as bad as it seems. I have a plan that may allow Oklas to leave much sooner.'

Stasia's balcony overlooked the courtyard separating the dormitories. Situated on the top floor of the staff block, it also offered a view of the sunlit edge of the lake and the trees beyond. Stasia emerged from her room, now wearing a fleecy pale gown. Her short tendrils were in disarray; she was never as beautiful as when she was a little ruffled. Emis had been looking forward to spending the segeind here with her. But with his mood still sour from the meeting, he felt like doing little more than glowering into his mug of kahv.

Closing her balcony door, Stasia fetched her mug from the counter and joined Emis in the high-ceilinged living room. She never drank kahv in the segeinds; her hot drink looked similar to the frothy concoction Emis had bought Oklas.

She caught him looking at the steaming drink in her hands. 'Would you like a taste?' she offered.

'All right.' Emis set down his mug and sipped from hers. The drink was sweet, mildly spicy, and just underneath that was something sharp on his tongue. This definitely wasn't something you'd give to a tideling.

'After today, I needed this,' said Stasia, reaching for an innocuous glass bottle on the table. 'You look like you could do with a helping yourself.'

He held out his mug, and she added a liberal shot of bitters to his kahv.

'I was surprised when Advisor Pawel told me you had taken only Oklas out for the segment,' said Stasia, sitting next to Emis on a sofa much comfier than the one in the staff room. 'Usually, you start with a group and narrow down from there.'

Emis sighed. 'That sounds like me. Afraid to give anyone too much time in case a better candidate comes along.'

'It would be easier if you did broaden your search, consider some juveniles a little older than Oklas. But you don't want to, do you?'

'No, Stas. I need to trust my instincts on this. I've found the person I came for.'

'I could see you'd made up your mind. The governors' resistance only makes you want Oklas all the more.' She gave a tired smile. 'You know I only played down his talents to improve your chances of getting him?'

Emis nodded, and Stasia continued, 'Oklas has an uncommon curiosity. He wants to understand the "why" of things.'

'More than that,' added Emis, 'he instinctively enhances the mood of a room, a skill that's somewhat undervalued in this region.'

'It is, unfortunately.'

'Which is why he isn't suited to a career in Dras Sayve,' said Emis, stretching an arm over the backrest of Stasia's seat. 'I just hope the governors let him go. He'd hate to be stuck biding his time while his harvestmates get on with their lives.' He brushed Stasia's shoulder. 'I'm eager to hear this plan of yours. You seem so sure you'll get them to relent.'

'Well, I can't promise anything, but you met only three of the eight governors today. That gives you another five to win over, and Inger is already on your side.' She studied him. 'How much longer will you stay here?'

'For the rest of this phase.'

'Strange that the two governors close to Valenska made it today and the others didn't,' said Stasia, nestling back into Emis's reach. 'I don't know if he arranged it that way. I am concerned about some of our leaders. They're becoming insular. Paranoid, even. Perhaps we have too little to worry about here?'

'It's not just here. The Pentarchy were the first to close their borders to outsiders. I almost feel sorry for them. When you start thinking everyone is trying to steal from you, you deprive yourself of so much.'

Quiet moments went by before Stasia spoke again. 'I will arrange a time later this week for the other governors to meet Oklas and speak with some of his teachers. They will see he's not exactly a conventional Sayvian. Even those against the idea of him travelling may decide that he is better off somewhere else. Afterwards, you can invite them aboard your watercraft as an act of goodwill. I will send my staff ahead of time to help you cater to them. They will want to see you can continue exposing Oklas to our foods and customs.'

'If that's what it takes to convince them,' said Emis with a resigned sigh.

'Let's see you come up with something better, then.'

'It's a brilliant plan, Stas – discreet. I was just going to abduct him.'

The laughter lines deepened in her blue cheeks, and she gave him a reproving tap on the wrist. 'Let's hope it doesn't come to that.'

Emis frowned. 'Do you think the other fifth-formers will be disappointed that I didn't take them on the outing today?'

'It depends how many of them saw Oklas leave with you,' replied Stasia. 'There's inevitably some jealousy at that age. I know Bystry wants to study under someone noteworthy.'

'If she wants someone important to emulate, she needn't look further than you.'

Stasia almost smiled and quickly gulped down the last of her spiked drink.

'All those I met in Form 5 yesterday would make good protégés,' admitted Emis. 'But I've already taught those who are clever and ambitious. That's just the problem; many Praemor knyads already have a fixed vision for their lives. Nothing I show them will alter the destination they already have in mind.'

'Some people make their own opportunities. Others need someone to help them know what they want.' Stasia placed her slender hand over Emis's much larger one. 'I think you'd be good for Oklas. He reminds me of you: restless. I thought that would either draw you to him or put you off.'

'We're quite different, really,' said Emis. 'He's got better manners for a start. I couldn't know what I wanted until I'd tried a bit of everything, and I had to travel the moon to do that. After a while, Knyadrea started feeling small. Like every clan was much the same as the next. Oklas would benefit from travel, but he doesn't need me to show him the world; he can explore it all from inside his mind. I think he's more like you, Stas.'

'Me?' she asked laughingly.

'You may have been too smart to get into trouble, but you were never boring. You introduced me to new ways of looking at things I thought I knew.'

'My imagination isn't nearly as boundless as Oklas's.'

'You've fostered his love of learning – the juve devours data and books.' Emis leaned forwards, resting a hand on his knee. 'But think of how much he could achieve if someone showed him how to bring his ideas into reality. I could advise him on which goals to pursue and introduce him to the people and systems that can make them happen. I don't want to teach him merely to thrive in the world as it is. I want to see him instigate change.'

Stasia tipped her head to one side. The soft light from the windows warmed her skin tone, and the lines in her brow, etched by years of responsibility, grew faint. 'When you arrived here this time, something felt different,' she observed. 'Oklas isn't just another protégé to you, is he?'

'No.' Emis got up and took a few slow steps towards the window, his hands in his pockets. 'I'm starting to feel my age, Stas – I don't expect you can relate, brimming with youth as you are.' The subdued flattery earned him a snort from her, and he continued. 'I'm wondering what the next half of my life might hold. I've done well for myself, but I don't want to leave my fortune to the Rindarian Estate or some charity I have no connection to. I want someone to take my legacy and make it aer own, to go even further with it.'

Stasia's inquiring expression softened. 'It sounds like you yearn for what no knyad can have ... an heir.'

'If you can conceive of such a thing,' said Emis with a gentle chuckle. 'I'd like to know my reasons for teaching, rather than what I teach will live on.'

Stasia picked up the empty mugs and made towards the kitchen. 'You both have a way of getting around me,' she said with a forced airiness. 'It's probably for the best if you take Oklas off my hands.'

Though slightly built, Stasia tackled every task with vigour. But, right now, she looked frail, almost sad. Emis came up behind her and placed a hand on her shoulder.

'I shouldn't get attached to any of them – it's unprofessional.' Her voice wavered, and she turned from Emis. 'I couldn't ask for a better calling, preparing tidelings for life on Dras Sayve. But I never get close enough to bond with them. I sometimes envy you for that. Oklas isn't truly happy here, and I can't give him what he needs.'

'I'll make sure he doesn't forget where he comes from,' Emis assured her, 'doesn't forget you.'

She reached to squeeze his hand on her shoulder. 'I thought he'd make a good teacher or dormitory advisor. You've seen how he is with the tidelings.' She gave a teary laugh. 'But he's not one for enforcing rules. Or routines.'

'You and your team have raised him well. I'll take over from here; turn him into someone you can be proud of.'

She sniffed, wiping her cheek. 'I'm already proud of him.'

Emis wrapped both arms around her and let her dry her face in his coat. Stasia's emotions were never far below the surface, but it wasn't proper for a Sayvian to display them too readily, and she strove to maintain her composure. During their time at the Drassian Academy, Emis had delighted in provoking her. She was right to call him an oaf back then. He much preferred these happy tears to the frustrated kind he used to elicit from her. That she now felt safe in his presence was his finest achievement.

'It's funny,' said Emis, 'I searched my home clan for an heir, but I couldn't find the right person in all of Dras Rindar.'

Stasia pulled away and straightened, looking up at him.

'Then I come here' – he stroked back the tendrils from her forehead – 'and Dras Sayve always seems to ... you always show me the way, Stas. Oklas is coming with me, I know it. This is meant to be.'

She folded back the lapel of Emis's coat. 'Fate isn't something many here believe in. But I want to. Adecai, I want to believe.'

The years between them melted away, and for one blissful moment, Emis and Stasia were as they had been on their best segs at the Drassian Academy: free of concerns and hopeful about what the future might hold.

CHAPTER 7

Ocean-bound

I T DIDN'T TAKE MUCH work to make the upper decks of the Cabin Cruiser presentable; Emis was used to entertaining on the vessel. But he was grateful to have Stasia's caterers aboard as his cook from Dalga wasn't familiar with Sayvian dishes. If there was anything Emis had learned in all his years as a diplomat, it was that presenting people with the right meals was essential to smoothing inter-clan relations. After a segment of frantic preparations, Emis was ready for his second meeting with the governors.

At the wharf, a distinguished group awaited him. The knyads differed in stature and wore garments, plain and patterned, ranging from soft neutrals to shimmering deep purple. Oklas was also there, neatly dressed in his dormitory uniform. Emis plastered an eager host's smile on his face and walked to the base of the gangway, welcoming aboard Advisor Pawel; six governors; senior presumptives Katoka and Valenska; and Oklas. While his staff showed the party through to the entertainment deck, Stasia caught Emis alone on the gangway.

'It's gone well so far,' she said, leaning close to his ear as the rumble of waves sounded around them. 'I had Oklas show the governors around the classrooms while they interviewed him. Few juveniles enjoy having an audience as much as he does. I think he exhausted Governor Ustal – who had to leave with Inger for another event – but the others are impressed with his communication skills.' She touched Emis's arm, possibly to reassure him or to steady herself as the gangway rocked. 'You still have to contend with Burza, but I've been doing my best to keep her and Valenska separate. If all goes well, Oklas should be allowed to leave as soon as he's graduated.'

'If all goes well,' repeated Emis, loosening his shirt collar.

'You don't need to put on a show here; Dras Sayve is a second home to you. I know you can answer any of their questions. When we go inside, talk to Governor Cintia, the tall knyad with the night-blue skin. She has the most authority and will likely be the deciding vote.'

'What will she want to hear?'

'You told me you'd see to all Oklas's needs,' answered Stasia. 'Tell her that Dras Sayve can keep his allowance. It'll earn you her trust.'

The pair made their way onto the deck and joined the others.

In the middle of the watercraft's three decks was the main lounge. The interior of the Rindarian Cabin Cruiser was much smaller than some of Emis's land-bound properties, but the watercraft's amenities interested the Sayvians, many of whom were not well-travelled. Though outnumbered by the adults, Oklas remained confident and good-humoured, joking that he had thought he was in trouble when his elder called for him earlier that segment. Emis guided him and Stasia to the bridge, where he left them with Captain Senga. That would keep the juvenile out of mischief and give Emis time to mingle with his other guests.

Senga sailed them up the coast, away from the tideling cove. The window walls of the entertainment deck offered panoramic views of the sea and shore; billowing clouds brought the landscape to life, sending spectral shadows swooping over the tree-dusted mountains. In the background, a gentle acoustic melody played.

Emis had a talent for remembering names and had learned just enough about each of the guests that he could engage them in brief, lively conversations. It wasn't long before he had them recounting favourite memories, even laughing at the sensation of being on the water again for the first time in years. The sea had that effect on knyads. They belonged here.

He even impressed the stately Governor Cintia and Katoka with stories of his visits to the planet side of the moon. Cintia in particular was enthralled by tales of the ancient civilisation of Rhestatyn, and when she started asking what Emis would show Oklas there, he knew he had won her support. At her prompting, he gave a detailed account of his plans for Oklas's education.

The breeze from yesterday had died down, but the sea was still choppier than when Emis had arrived in Dras Sayve. The watercraft rode the peaks and troughs of waves with little effort. Though the Cabin Cruiser was large enough to stabilise the rocking motion, Valenska fell ill and retired to a spare cabin. Only Burza seemed to notice his absence. While not seasick, she looked miserable, sitting in a corner with her back turned to the windows. Emis signalled Senga to set sail back towards the harbour.

Satisfied that the hour he had spent with the governors had gone smoothly, Emis excused himself and went to look for Oklas and Stasia. He found them on the lower deck, at the stern. A sea mist was rolling off the waves, and Stasia pointed out the angled sunlight beaming off the glass fronts of some buildings. They were laughing about something. Neither had noticed Emis, and he held back for a while, smiling to himself as he watched them have a rare moment together.

Not all knyads in a clan resembled one another, but standing side by side, Stasia and Oklas looked like two figures shaped by the same forces. They were of a similar build, and the juvenile stood only a little taller than his elder. Their mouths curved into the same smiles, bright against their cloudy-blue complexions. Stasia turned and caught Emis's eye. She stepped back for Emis to come between her and Oklas.

'I wouldn't want to interrupt the fun you two are having there,' he said as he approached the pair.

'Not at all,' said Stasia. 'We noticed the watercraft turn around. Is everything all right?' She looked at Emis pointedly.

'The trip was just as we hoped it would be,' he replied, suppressing a chuckle as he noticed Oklas watching them, trying to decipher the hidden meaning in the exchange. The juvenile missed nothing. 'We're heading back now,' Emis continued. 'I think everyone is enjoying the ride, except for Valenska, perhaps. There can't be enough seawater in his blood.'

'The poor knyad,' said Stasia. 'I'd better go and see to him. I brought along some medication for queasiness.'

She patted Oklas's upper arm before leaving. It was Emis's turn to speak with him.

Taking Stasia's place beside the juvenile, Emis clasped his hands together on the gunwale in front of him. 'Oklas, there's a reason I invited you and the governors here today.'

'Did they grant me permission to go on your next trip?'

'They're uh … coming around to the idea. You have your elder to thank for that. She has been working on them. I suppose your harvestmates have been speculating my reason for being here?'

'They say you tutor people.'

Emis nodded. 'I'd like to have you aboard – but not just as a porter on a single trip. I want to offer you more than any juvenile who has studied with me.'

Emis relayed what he had discussed with Stasia, emphasising learning opportunities. He did not bring up his hopes to make Oklas his heir. The juvenile was too young to bear such expectations, and Emis did not want to rob him of the motivation to excel in his own right.

Oklas listened intently, looking into the waves as Emis spoke and stammering a quiet 'thank you' when he finished.

'I understand it's a lot to take in,' said Emis, craning his neck to meet Oklas's downcast eyes.

'It's amazing. Everything I could have hoped for,' said the juvenile, recovering his voice. He gave a tight smile. 'No one's ever chosen me, out of all my harvestmates, for anything like this before.'

'And that troubles you?'

'It's just ... I haven't done much apart from them. I could be gone a long time.'

'Yes. If you choose to come with me – and the choice is yours – it would set you up for a life on the move. When I'm not at sea or visiting clans, I reside in cities abroad. It would be very different from Dras Sayve.'

Oklas gripped the gunwale and nodded, his tendrils falling over his eyes.

'So many adults have been voicing their opinions on this matter, having a say in your future,' said Emis, leaning his back against the gunwale. 'But it's for you to decide, Oklas; I don't expect your answer today. Remember, you can't disappoint me. Even if it turns out this isn't what you want, we can still keep in touch.'

Oklas looked up. 'Would I be able to visit the Dras Channel?'

'At least once a year if you like.'

'And what would you teach me?'

'Anything that catches your interest. I teach every subject the Dras Channel has to offer and more. After a few years, when you decide on a field that interests you, I will tailor your course to prepare you for an academy of your choosing.'

Oklas held Emis's gaze. Haltingly, he asked, 'How am I to repay you for all this?'

Emis smiled inwardly – he really did have the right juvenile. Beneath Oklas's bright-eyed enthusiasm was a surprising shrewdness, a willingness to examine every facet of an opportunity.

Scratching his chin, Emis replied, 'You would help the crew with some chores, of course, but I'd mainly require your assistance as my envoy on long trips. For this reason, I would include diplomacy as a compulsory subject when tutoring you. I know you aren't keen on politics, but I'd like you to give it a chance.'

'It's not that I don't like it,' said Oklas, stumbling as the watercraft rolled into the trough of a wave. 'I just don't know if I'd be any good at it.'

'You already are.' Emis bent his knees, keeping his balance as the watercraft navigated a choppy reach. 'In all the time we spent together, I've been testing you. You are a natural conversationalist, well-read on a broad range of subjects. And you made me, an outsider, feel welcome here, sharing your culture with me and asking about mine.'

'But I'm not a leader. People look to Bystry to organise group assignments.'

'Both of you are quick to identify people's strengths. But there's more to leadership than telling people what to do. You have to make them feel appreciated for their efforts; show them a good time. Do you think you can manage that?'

Oklas adjusted his posture to appear confident, but he wore Emis's comments like a suit he hadn't quite grown into.

'Come, let me show you around the watercraft,' said Emis, walking up the deck towards the bow. 'I spend phases at sea between cities. You might take a while to adjust to life on the water.'

'Surely all knyads are adapted for it?' said Oklas, following him. 'We come from the sea, after all.'

'Not all knyads find bobbing on the surface as natural as swimming below. It's encouraging that you're holding up well on this trip, but the weather isn't always this calm.'

'Are you trying to scare me off, kyr?'

'I'm priming your expectations. Every good thing has its drawbacks.'

Emis led Oklas through a hatch leading to the watercraft's interior. They walked the main corridor, passing Emis's study and the lounge, where the visitors were still.

'There are a lot of doors here,' said the juvenile. 'Do all your crew members have their own cabins?'

'Yes, and if you were to stay here, you'd have a cabin too.' Emis climbed the stairwell to the third floor and opened the first cabin door after the landing.

Oklas's mouth dropped open.

An oval table and low sofas were arranged along the sides of a sunken floor. Beyond the bed and adjustable desk, the far side of the cabin opened out onto large, curving window walls with handrails at their bases. An en suite bathroom lay behind frosted glass doors. The juvenile took awed steps into the space, tilting his head back.

Emis lived to share the luxuries he could easily take for granted with young knyads like Oklas. Most Praemor juveniles were hard to satisfy, let alone impress, but Sayvians were not spoilt. Although Dras Sayve was a relatively wealthy clan, they raised tidelings to share rooms and belongings.

'There's so much space.' Oklas skipped over to the windows. 'Dras Sayve looks completely different at sea.'

As the watercraft returned to the harbour, the pale shoreside buildings along the coast rose out of the water like the white wings of seabirds.

Oklas sunk onto the bed and asked, 'What is it like waking up and looking outside to see a new clan waiting for you?'

'Depends where I am.' Emis lowered himself onto the opposite end of the bed and watched the scenery drift by. 'Each coast is different, as are the knyads who live there.'

'What are the Orta clans like?'

It shouldn't have surprised Emis that Oklas's teachers had taught him little about the lower strata, focusing instead on clans they considered their equals.

He answered, 'You'd be surprised at what some can do with virtually no technology. Don't make the mistake I did – thinking you already live at the pinnacle of civilisation. Knyads elsewhere will always have something to teach you.'

Oklas laughed. 'I'd be disappointed if everyone saw things as Sayvians do.'

'Many are of a more spiritual persuasion than we in the Dras Channel are,' noted Emis. 'With faith alone, some of them do things I can't explain. Adecai's intervention is as real to them as the sea beneath this watercraft.'

'Who is Adecai?'

'Someone who appears to knyads in different guises, offering wisdom or performing miracles. Many consider Aer to be our Creator.'

Swinging his knees onto the bed, Oklas turned to face Emis. 'I've heard resyn can do miraculous things, but my teachers say it's only good for powering technology.'

'Resyn is certainly a high-quality alternative to the common fulmenum cell,' said Emis, 'but that is not to say it's without mystical properties.'

Oklas arched an eyebrow at him.

Emis meandered to the nearby table and retrieved a nut from a bowl. 'Take this dentricle, for instance,' he said, holding it up for Oklas to see. 'You have the serrated shell – one layer of reality – but there is also the seed inside. Though the seed is hidden, it is perhaps the most important part of the nut.' Using a plier-shaped nutcracker from the bowl, Emis broke through the hard shell. 'A gifted few can crack open reality and access the supernatural. Those who do that are called resyn-crafters.'

'There's not much material in the library about resyn-craft,' said Oklas, hopping to his feet and joining Emis at the table. 'Most people here say it's a thing of folklore; that practitioners are frauds. But if that is all they are, why hide information about them?'

Emis considered the juvenile. 'Sayvians possess many admirable qualities,' he began. 'Few can match their rigorous intellect, but some mysteries can't be investigated with the mind alone. I think that scares them. I daresay your teachers don't want you getting fanciful ideas about testing for an aptitude in resyncraft.'

In a hushed tone, Oklas asked, 'You can study resyncraft?'

'Those who pass the test can. But there's more to it than cracking a nut – I can tell you.' Emis placed a hand on the juvenile's back and guided him to the cabin door. 'Only a rare few possess the gift. Most of us have to make do with the shell.'

Oklas glanced back at the nutcracker on the table. 'Then I'll just have to make the tools to crack it for me.'

Emis laughed. 'I look forward to seeing you do that. That attitude will take you far, Oklas.'

They returned to the first-floor deck and walked to the prow, facing the breeze. Shielding his eyes from the sun, Emis could make out the edge of the wharf jutting into the sea.

'What happens next?' asked Oklas.

Emis turned to face his young ward. 'We're still sorting out the details with the governors. For now, you need only focus on your remaining tests and assignments. I will come back for you next revolution.'

Signalling Sophistication

AFTER A HASTY TRIP to Wydion on the border of Knyadrea's planet-facing side and a stopover at Dras Rindar to restock supplies, Emis was back in Dras Sayve. For young Oklas, however, it seemed the revolution hadn't passed quickly enough. According to Stasia, he had spent the past phase visiting the wharf each median and staring out to sea, searching for the slightest hint of a cabin cruiser on the dark horizon. His teachers had been stunned by the newfound enthusiasm with which he had taken to his studies. In his final tests, he scored better results than anyone had expected. All he had needed was an incentive to apply himself.

Presently, Emis was escorting Oklas out of a clothing shop in Dras Sayve's town centre. Ordinarily, Emis delighted in a spot of shopping, but this expedition had proved slightly disappointing. It was more overcast than his previous visit to the island, even though he had arrived a little later in the light phase. At this time of year, the shops here stocked little besides long-sleeved shirts, jackets, and padded coats. Oklas would need something lighter for where they were headed next. The Litusian continent to the southwest was much warmer. Perhaps Emis should have bought some garments while he was in Rindar. But then, he hadn't known the juvenile's measurements.

'We could go to the tailor's,' suggested Oklas pointing across the street.

Emis shook his head. 'There isn't time for us to come back here and collect the garments tomorrow. It can wait until we reach the continent. We'll arrive in the dark, which should give us time to find something for the lunar day.'

Oklas looked at the bulging trolly bag before him. 'All this must be expensive. I may not need anything more. Especially since I already have clothes for the warm phases.' The juve was strangely attached to the clothes provided by his dormitory. They were comfortable and neat but plain.

'Oklas, while you are welcome to wear them in your cabin, you will need something smarter for our outings. You are a sophisticated young knyad; you signal this with the right wardrobe.' Emis turned on the spot, scanning the glassy mainsail-shaped towers to find his bearings. 'Now, perhaps we should find you some pairs of shoes.'

Emis and Oklas passed a track-footed automaton diligently clearing snow with its scooped claws and arrived at Skórei, the best shoe shop in Dras Sayve. The beetle-like automaton whirred to one side, rolling a large snowball to the slushy collection it had amassed outside the entrance. At their approach, the doors slid open and out walked three knyads. Oklas skidded to hide behind Emis as Bystry, Casimir, and an ungainly juvenile rounded the corner. He had involved his friends in several fun activities with Emis over the past few segments, but this trip was to be kept secret. It seemed Oklas didn't want them watching Emis buy him items their allowances couldn't cover. Emis's size, while impressive enough to obscure his ward, also had a way of drawing attention.

'Hello, Master Rindar,' said Bystry and Casimir in unison, visibly surprised to see him alone.

'You all right back there, Oklas?' asked the third juvenile dreamily, standing on tiptoe to glimpse past Emis's shoulder.

'Hello, Ranek,' he replied, subdued.

Ranek pointed to the trolly bag. 'What do you have in there?'

'Oh, it's uh …'

'He's clearly helping Master Rindar carry his purchases,' cut in Bystry. 'It's not for us to pry into an adult's business.'

'I assure you my loot is not nearly as dazzling as yours, Ranek,' said Emis, gesturing at the glittering boots peeping from her parcel. He never thought he'd see Sayvian footwear in such vibrant colours.

'That's probably true,' she agreed with a faraway look in her large green eyes. 'These aren't new. I only came here to buy the shoelaces. I glued on the sequins myself.'

A tram drew up on the other side of the street. 'Will we see you at supper, Oklas?' asked Casimir as he tugged Ranek by the sleeve.

'I'll be there.'

The pair of them jogged over to the tram.

'You're not going with them?' asked Emis, tilting his head at Bystry.

She shuddered. 'Certainly not. We just left the shop at the same time.'

'Bystry doesn't usually keep their company,' explained Oklas in a lofty tone, turning from Emis to her. 'Where are Edurne and Nasek?'

'Home today. I came into town on my own. So, Oklas, are those *your* new clothes in there?'

'N-no,' he replied unconvincingly.

'Don't worry; I won't tell anyone. Not that your friends would care what Master Rindar buys you for your trip. They wouldn't know good clothes if they saw them.' She inclined her head at Emis. 'I'm glad you're making him presentable, kyr.' Returning to Oklas and elbowing him in the ribs, she added, 'I can't have you embarrassing me while you're overseas.'

'You have an eye for trends, Bystry,' said Emis. 'Would you like to help your harvestmate choose his shoes? Find him something suitable, and I'll buy you a pair too.'

Oklas groaned as Bystry eagerly accepted Emis's challenge. She swiftly led them to the sections of the shop Emis was looking for. She knew every shelf in Skórei's aisles; it was as if she worked there. Emis had Oklas try on a range of formal lace-up shoes and more casual pairs. Bystry provided a valuable third perspective when differences of opinion arose. In most cases, she sided with Emis's choice of footwear, though she also defended one of Oklas's choices. While she didn't like the cut of his high-top shoes, she admitted that they suited him.

'So what are your plans for the future, Bystry?' asked Emis, watching her try on a pair of charcoal-coloured boots with pointed toes.

'I'll be staying in town while I complete my secondaries. I came here to sign up for student accommodation today.'

'And you've decided on your subjects?'

'Oh, yes. I tailored my selection to meet the requirements for the Governors' Program at the Drassian Academy.'

With reluctant admiration, Oklas added, 'Even in Form 1, Bystry knew that's what she wanted to study.'

'Well, if today is anything to go by, future peers will benefit from your solid counsel,' Emis told Bystry.

She smiled and took her harvestmate by the hand. 'We all knew you'd be the first to leave, Oklas.' Swallowing hard, she continued, 'I don't want to live anywhere else, but I'd like to travel someday, so don't muck this up.'

Oklas pulled her into a hug, and she made a strangled sound.

'Maybe I can invite all of you to visit me in another clan?' he suggested, stepping back.

Bystry gave him a withering look. 'That'll never happen. We can barely keep everyone together in the same dormitory. But If you become an ambassador to one of the big cities, you'll have to return to Dras Sayve occasionally.' She smirked. 'Maybe you will finally listen to me if I'm the one you're reporting back to.'

'Now *that's* something that will never happen,' retorted Oklas, and Bystry rolled her eyes. Grinning, he continued, 'I don't see myself as an ambassador' – he glanced over his shoulder at Emis – 'but I'm not ruling out politics altogether.'

The juveniles continued chatting while Emis paid for their goods. This was as new to him as it was to Oklas; his previous students had all come prepared with some belongings of their own. A juvenile fresh from the dormitories required more coordination than anticipated. It was just as well that Emis liked a challenge.

It was the segment of Oklas's departure, and the weather had cleared. A brisk, salty breeze had picked up at the harbour, and foamy clouds dappled the blue sky. Gathered at the wharf were Oklas's harvestmates, joined by the dormitory staff members and some teachers. Kosta and Lehel came down the gangway, having helped Oklas carry the last of his luggage aboard. The juveniles crowded Oklas, each gripping his arm in turn. Ranek ruffled his tendrils, and Jedrik clapped him on the back.

From the port side of the watercraft, Emis watched the activity below. He kept his distance so as not to interrupt the goodbyes. Eventually, Stasia followed Oklas up the gangway. When they reached the top, she placed her hands on the juvenile's shoulders, lifting her pointed chin to appraise him. 'Now, if there is anything you need – anything to make you feel more at home – you will send a message to my office, won't you?'

Oklas nodded, then Stasia folded her arms around him, and he sank into her embrace. Both were teary-eyed; perhaps Stasia had come up here just for a moment alone with him?

She then walked up to Emis, who bent to hug her too. 'Safe travels, dear one,' she said, threading her hand through his tendrils.

'Take care of yourself, Stas. We'll be back for a visit before you know it.'

The Cabin Cruiser's engines hummed to life. From the stern, Oklas waved to all who had come to see him off. Emis stood at the juvenile's side, his gaze lingering on Stasia until she blended into the crowd. Gradually, the wharf and conifers shrunk in the distance. Soon, even the snow-capped mountains of Dras Sayve looked like no more than cresting breakers on the horizon.

Oklas folded his arms on the gunwale at the side of the watercraft, staring at the last traces of his clan.

'Taking it all in, are you?' asked Emis.

'I spent so much time wishing I was somewhere else,' replied Oklas. 'I never thought I'd miss home. But I do now.' He clutched at the jacket fabric over his chest. 'No place will shape me the way Dras Sayve has. I want to remember every detail of it.'

'You really think you are done growing, done changing?'

'I suppose not.'

'Time changes things more than distance. Even your harvestmates who stay behind won't remain the same. They will enter different careers; choose different paths in life.'

'It's going to be strange,' said Oklas, 'not seeing them every seg.'

Emis strode across the deck. 'You don't seem to have trouble making new friends.'

'I just didn't think about what it would feel like to leave the old ones behind. This is all happening so quickly.'

It was difficult for every tideling to transition into this phase of life. Even the most well-prepared among them could only guess what it meant to be a juvenile. After several decades, Emis still didn't know exactly what it meant to be a grown knyad.

'You know, Oklas, you may be my only protégé at this time. But you will have many opportunities to meet other people your age in a variety of programs.'

He turned his back on the vanishing island, looking out to sea. 'Every new encounter will increase what is already inside you,' he continued. 'Soon, you will find you have much to give to everyone you meet.'

Oklas didn't say anything, but some cheer returned to his expression. The clear blue of the open ocean brought out the same hue in his eyes. Less than a hundred alkar away, an armoured drassyr's head and plated back rose from the waves. Oklas jumped at the sight of it, dissolving into delighted laughter. Soon, Emis was laughing too. Every new venture was made up of moments like this. Although Emis couldn't say what Oklas's moments with him would amount to, he would use each for all it was worth.

Acknowledgements

COMING-OF-AGE TALES ARE SELDOM told from an adult mentor's perspective. But Emis had a robust voice that needed to be heard, and he could take us into corners of Sayvian society that others could not. Allowing him to tell an insider's story felt natural.

The Tidelings of Dras Sayve grew out of the backstory I had developed for Oklas, one of the two protagonists in *Far Removed*. There was enough material to draw on for a short story, but I didn't want the prequel to feel like a vehicle for exposition. Insights into Sayvian culture and references to my duology had to orbit a theme that exerted a strong gravitational pull. The mentor-apprentice relationship between Oklas and Emis drew me in and became the centrepiece of this story. I dedicated *Tidelings* to mentors because I will never forget the moments when a teacher identified a quality in me that I could not yet see.

We all keep alternating between the roles of student and mentor. One person I learned from is Rachel Bowdler, my proofreader on this novelette. I found her on social media after noticing fellow writers recommend her editing services. Rachel thoroughly cleaned up my comma placement and improved the clarity of my prose. If you are keen on cosy romances with some diversity, look up her books; she is a prolific author.

Thank you to the newsletter subscribers who read *Tidelings* while it was still an early draft. I am also grateful for the returning readers who picked up this title after reading *Far Removed*. As I continue writing the sequel to that novel, I am excited to notice some themes echoing in my reread of *Tidelings*. This cosy novelette is one book I can share with my parents. I should warn those who have not yet read *Far Removed* that, tonally, it departs from the lightheartedness of *Tidelings*. It is a character-driven horror story, portraying losses of varying kinds. But I don't leave characters in pits of despair for long, and my duology will also take you into the heart of the vivid, complex world that is Knyadrea.

Finally, ratings and reviews are always welcome as they greatly help to extend a book's reach. Stories are only as alive as the people who talk about them.

Charismatic and innovative, Oklas Sayve has risen to prominence in Apidecca, the moon's capital city. A politician and college director, he has the resources to effect the changes he envisions for the world. But the sovereigns he serves oppose him at every turn and his status cannot protect the low-strata students attending his college. After a young knyad is wrongly linked to insurgent activity, Oklas must find a way to smuggle her out of the city while hiding his involvement from the authorities.

Below the grand Assembly Chambers, a knyad in a mask sculpts, grasping for scraps of beauty in her shrinking world. Years ago, Prismer made a costly mistake and now has only her job at the projection booth and a few special interests to fill her days. But it is not her sculptures that draw the attention of a powerful client, and she is soon met with a request to undertake a dangerous mission. Will she answer the call and risk losing the little she has left?

Mysteries surface. A supernatural substance is used in corrupt ways. As identities shift and predicaments are reshuffled, what alliances might be forged?

About the Author

MOUNTAINS, SEA AND URBAN sprawl: these are as much a part of imaginary worlds as the place where Coe Lansdell lives, at the tip of Africa. Her dogs ensure she is exercised daily. Encounters with birdlife and fynbos on weekends are essential to her creativity. For best results, she should be left to soak in a rock pool at least once a month. Most days, she can be found in her home office, wearing her headphones to drown out the howling southeasterly wind.

Author website:
https://cblansdell.com/links/

www.ingramcontent.com/pod-product-compliance
Lightning Source LLC
Chambersburg PA
CBHW061108100726
47911CB00012B/455